An eye for an eye

Author: Lorimer, Janet.
Reading Level: 4.3 UG
.O
R QUIZ# 43648

D0629349

An Eye
for an Eye

Janet Lorimer

SADDLEBACK
PAGETURNERS

• SPY •

PAGETURNERS

Development and Production: Laurel Associates, Inc.
Cover Illustrator: Black Eagle Productions

Copyright © 2001 by Saddleback Publishing, Inc. All rights reserved.
No part of this publication may be reproduced or transmitted in any
form without permission in writing from the publisher. Reproduction
of any part of this book, through photocopy, recording, or any
electronic or mechanical retrieval system, without the written
permission of the publisher, is an infringement of copyright law.

Three Watson
Irvine, CA 92618-2767

E-Mail: info@sdlback.com
Website: www.sdlback.com

ISBN 1-56254-137-4

Printed in the United States of America
05 04 03 02   9 8 7 6 5 4 3 2 1

CONTENTS

Chapter 1

Sandy Norris took a deep breath, closed her eyes, and concentrated. Her right hand moved lightly over the large brown envelope on the table in front of her. Little by little, her breathing slowed.

Sitting across the table from Sandy, Detective Sam Kennedy leaned forward, watching her closely.

All at once, Sandy slumped forward. Her hand continued to make a circular motion over the envelope. Only the movement of her hand told Sam that she was still awake.

The small room they were in was rectangular, small, and bare. Just one thing broke up the monotony of the décor—a large mirror on the far wall. Behind the one-way mirror stood a man in a dark suit. He, too, gazed fixedly at the curly-haired young woman.

Suddenly, she gasped. "I'm in the country," she said. A slight frown drew her eyebrows together, and she tilted her head to one side. "I'm in the foothills, not on a main highway. I see a dirt road leading into this place. Dry grass. A fence is falling down, and there's a barn with big holes in the roof. No one's been in this place for a long time."

Her hand began to move faster, and her breathing speeded up. "I'm going into the barn."

Then she paused again, frowning. Her face crumpled and tears began to trickle out from under her lashes. "I'm so scared," Sandy said in a strange, high voice. She sounded like a frightened child. "Oh, please help me. I'm so scared and there's a—" Sandy gasped, then cried out, "A *snake*! I see it. It's—"

Sam Kennedy's lips drew back over his gritted teeth.

Sandy huddled down in the chair. "It's too dark in here . . . I'm scared," she whimpered in the childish voice. "I'm so tired. Mommy? Where are you? Daddy, why did you leave me here alone? Mommy? Daddy? Help me!"

"Good work, Sandy," Sam growled. "Now tell me where you are?"

Sandy groaned and straightened up in her chair. A moment later she opened her eyes. She blinked, shook her head, and then gazed at Sam. "I need a map."

He pulled a map from his jacket pocket and handed it to her. Sandy unfolded it, spreading it between them on the table. Again she closed her eyes. And again her hand moved lightly over the surface. Then her finger pointed directly to a spot on the map.

She opened her eyes as Sam leaned over the table. Taking a closer look at the map, he said, "Hmmm. Carson Meadows. Seems to me there used to be a ranch there about 50 years ago. Now—"

"You'd better hurry," Sandy said softly. "I think the little girl is in or near a building—but there are snakes there. She's scared."

"I'll get right on it," Sam called over his shoulder as he bolted out of the room. With a sigh of relief, Sandy leaned back in her chair and closed her eyes. She looked worn out.

A moment later, Sam returned. He handed Sandy a glass of water. "How do you feel?" he asked.

Sandy opened one eye, grinned, and reached out for the glass. "I feel like someone just dropped me off a ten-story building," she said.

"Huh! If you fell off a building, you wouldn't feel a thing," Sam said with a twinkle in his eye. "You'd be giving harp lessons to the angels."

Sandy laughed. "Thanks for the support, Sam. You've always been my cheering section."

Sam grinned, but then grew serious.

"I contacted the search party and told them what you'd come up with. They said they'd get right on it."

"How long has that child been missing?" Sandy asked.

Sam's red face got a bit redder. As a seasoned detective with the Missing Persons Division, he'd hunted for *many* missing children. Sandy knew that he never stopped worrying that a lost child might not be found alive.

"Just a few hours," Sam said. "She was on a hiking trip with her family. Apparently, the little girl wandered off after lunch."

"How old is she?" Sandy asked.

"Six," Sam said quietly. He glanced over at the wall clock. "It'll be dark in another 15 minutes or so," he said. "We'd better not lose any time. The temperature has dropped below freezing the last couple of nights."

Sandy shivered. Then all of a sudden, she was again overwhelmed by the child's feelings. She felt wave after wave of fear, loneliness, and—Sandy struggled to identify the last powerful emotion.

Anger! The child was angry because her father had left her alone on the hillside! The little girl hadn't accidentally wandered away from her family. She'd been *deliberately* left behind. Sam wasn't telling Sandy the truth!

Chapter 2

Sandy felt sick—as if someone had punched her in the stomach. Sam was her *friend*, a person she trusted.

What was going on? It made no sense. Why would Sam Kennedy lie to her? They'd worked together on so many missing persons cases. What was different about this one? Sandy couldn't help feeling disappointed and betrayed.

The minutes ticked by. Finally, Sandy couldn't stand it. "Hey, can we get out of this room?" she said. "I feel like I'm trapped in a cell or something."

"Aw, come on," Sam teased. "Don't you like it in here? The lovely paint job? The comfortable furniture?"

Sandy made a face. "What *is* this room, anyway? Why are we here? It looks to me like an interrogation room."

"Would you believe that it is?" Sam grinned. But Sandy noticed that his laugh was forced. For some reason he seemed on edge.

"Okay, what's going on?" she asked.

"Nothing." Sam started tugging at his earlobe, a clear sign to Sandy that he was uncomfortable or nervous. "There was no other place to put you. Sorry about that."

Sandy gazed at him for a moment. She saw he was still lying—and that really hurt. She was certain that he'd never lied to her before.

"I need to wash my face," she said.

Sam nodded. "Okay, but hurry back. We might need you to . . ." His voice trailed away, and he looked even more uncomfortable. Sandy realized then that she had been put in this particular room for a *reason*.

As she stood up, she closed her eyes and focused her mind. Suddenly she felt as if someone had dumped a bucket of ice cubes down the back of her neck! She turned to see what was behind her. But there was nothing—except for the mirror on the far wall.

Sandy could *feel* his eyes. A man on the other side of that mirror was watching her. Worse yet, she was getting a bad feeling about the stranger.

She picked up her purse and left the room. As she walked down the hall toward the restroom, she noticed a door on her left. She was pretty sure it led into the observation room next door.

Sam had never put Sandy in an interrogation room before. Usually, she did her work in a comfortable office. "As comfortable as an office can get in a police station," she thought with a grin.

In the restroom, Sandy gazed at her reflection in the mirror. She looked tired. Well, she *was* tired! She'd come straight to the police station from class.

She remembered Sam's joke about

her giving harp lessons to the angels. Sandy smiled as she washed her face. She really *did* give harp lessons—but not to angels. Sandy was a full-time graduate student at the local university. Someday she planned to play with the city symphony. In the meantime, to help pay for her schooling, she also gave music lessons on the side.

And, of course, Sandy had another talent. She was psychic. As far back as she could remember, she'd been able to see things that no one else could see. And even as a small child, she'd often known in advance that certain things were going to happen.

Sandy was lucky. Her family didn't think of her as a freak. Her grandmother had also been a psychic. Gran told Sandy that she had a special gift—what Gran called "second sight."

"Some people are able to paint beautiful pictures," Gran said. "Some people can compose wonderful songs.

Those are their special gifts. *Your* gift, Sandy, is different—but it's still a very special gift."

Gran taught Sandy how to control her gift, and how to use it wisely to help other people.

When she grew up, however, Sandy learned not to say too much about her "second sight." She discovered that such talk frightened most of her friends. Some people thought of her as a monster. Others wanted to use her.

Then one day she'd had a vision about a lost child. The news story had been in the papers and on TV for nearly a week. Then suddenly, on her way to school one morning, Sandy "saw" the little boy. He was lying at the bottom of an abandoned well.

Chapter 3

Sandy drove straight to the site of the old well. It was in a huge empty field. She immediately called 911, and the boy was saved. Luckily, it turned out that the well was dry. But the child had been very close to death.

That case brought her face-to-face with gruff Detective Sam Kennedy for the first time. Sam did *not* believe in psychics. He did *not* believe in visions. And he certainly did *not* believe in "second sight." But Sandy's abilities eventually won him over.

The thing that impressed Sam was that Sandy would take no money for her work. "It's a gift that's meant to be shared," Sandy said. "I can't charge the people I help. Most of them are scared out of their wits, Sam. They've lost a loved one. I won't take advantage of desperate people."

There were a lot of cases Sandy wouldn't touch. She wouldn't help anyone who wanted to win money or hurt other people. Sam respected that. Over time, he had grown to know and respect Sandy as a person. They had become good friends.

Thinking about Sam brought Sandy back to the present. While she dried her face with a paper towel, she thought about the stranger in the observation room. She needed to know just who was watching her. And even more than that, she needed to know why Sam hadn't told her about it. Why was he cooperating with the stranger?

"It doesn't make sense," she thought, as she ran a comb through her short brown curls. "Sam really wanted me to find that little girl. He knows the way I work. Why would he hide someone in that observation room to spy on me?"

Maybe it was a cop from another precinct. But why wouldn't Sam have introduced them first? It *couldn't* be a reporter. Sam knew how much Sandy hated publicity.

"Something is going on," Sandy thought. "Sam knows about it and he doesn't like it."

Again, in a flash, the vision of the old barn came into Sandy's mind. It made her feel cold and scared. Then the vision disappeared. For a moment, feeling sick and weak, Sandy clung to the washbasin. Bit by bit, she forced herself to calm down, to focus on who she was and where.

When she felt stronger, Sandy left the restroom and headed down the hall. As she got closer to the door of the observation room, she couldn't shake the feeling of that dark presence. It was like nothing she had ever felt before. She grabbed the doorknob. But when her fingers touched the metal, Sandy cried out. It felt like a jolt of electric current had passed through her body!

At that moment, the door to the interrogation room opened. Sam stepped into the hall and looked at her curiously. "Hey, Sandy, what are you doing?"

She gazed at him blankly. Should she tell him about the shock she'd had when she touched the doorknob? She decided not to. "Oh, wrong door," she said. She tried to laugh, but the sound came out more like a gasp.

Sam frowned. "Are you all right?" he asked in a concerned voice.

"I—"

"Kennedy, phone call!" a young cop yelled from a doorway at the end of the hall.

Sam grabbed Sandy's hand and pulled her after him. "Come on. This may be it," he said.

In the office, he took the phone. "Kennedy," he snapped.

While he listened, Sandy held onto

the doorframe. For some reason, she was numb! She had no feelings one way or another, and she didn't understand why.

Sam turned. There was a wide grin on his face as he put his hand over the receiver. "They found the kid. She was plenty scared, but she's going to be okay," he said.

Sandy dropped into a chair. It was always a relief when the news was good.

Sam hung up. He pulled out his handkerchief and wiped his forehead. "Boy, that was a close call," he said. "I always worry myself sick until we find out for sure."

Sandy nodded. "Me, too," she said. "You never know. What if I'm too late? Or what if— By the way, Sam, what was in the brown envelope?"

"I forgot about the—" Sam started to sweat again. "I'd better go get—" He bolted from the room.

Sandy tore down the hall after him. She had had enough of this. "Sam, what is *up* with you today?" she demanded.

He stopped so suddenly that Sandy almost ran into him. When he opened the door of the interrogation room, Sandy peered around him.

A stranger was standing by the table, holding the envelope. The man looked straight at Sandy. His gaze chilled her. She felt as if someone had thrown a bucket of ice into her face.

No, she thought a moment later, it was worse than that. There was a feeling of darkness about the stranger—but the darkness was *inside* him. It was the only kind of darkness that terrified Sandy.

Chapter 4

The stranger smiled at Sandy. "Congratulations, Ms. Norris. You did a great job."

He stepped forward and handed her a small white card.

"MiraMed Technologies," she read out loud. "Eric Kemp." She looked up at the man. "You were watching me while I worked, weren't you?"

Kemp nodded. "When you looked at the mirror, I figured you knew I was here. But it was the only way—"

Sandy angrily whirled around and confronted the detective. "Sam, what's going on here?" she demanded.

Sam's face turned dark red. "I can see you're upset, but you've got to forgive me, kid. My boss insisted on it."

Kemp smiled, but Sandy sensed no real warmth or friendliness in his face. "It's a long story, Ms. Norris. Why don't we find a more comfortable place to chat. I imagine you must be hungry. How about dinner?"

"Smooth and slick," Sandy thought to herself. "Like a snake!" She cleared her throat and spoke in a frosty voice. "No thank you, Mr. Kemp. I believe my work is done here, so I'll be going home."

Kemp's eyes narrowed. Sandy sensed that he wasn't used to people going against his wishes. His hand tightened around the brown envelope.

"Excuse me," Sandy said, taking the envelope from his hand. She glanced at Sam, then tore the envelope open. Inside she found a blue hair ribbon and a child's sock.

Sandy was often given items like these when she looked for a missing person. The objects had to be something worn or handled by the person she searched for. Yet, as Sandy fingered the ribbon and the sock, she had an uncomfortable rush of mixed feelings. She frowned, gazing back and forth from one man to the other.

"Is this some kind of sick joke?" she said at last.

Sam stiffened. The corners of Eric Kemp's mouth twitched into a tiny smile. "What do you mean?" he asked.

Sandy was repelled by Kemp's smug face. She wanted to throw the ribbon and sock at him and walk away. Instead, she took a deep breath to calm her nerves.

"Something is very wrong with this picture," she said slowly. "I know the little girl was lost—I saw her. But I'm picking up other feelings, too. She wasn't really a *missing* child, was she?"

Sam sighed. "I don't want to lie to you, kid," he said, taking the sock and the ribbon from her. "These belong to a child, all right. And yeah—in a sense she was missing. Well, she *thought* she was. But yeah, kid, you're right. We were watching over her the whole time."

Sandy stared at Sam in horror. "Are you telling me you set this thing up? It was all a fake, and you knew it?"

"Don't blame Detective Kennedy," Kemp said. "He was only following orders. This was just a little test of your psychic abilities. My employer wanted to see for himself whether you're as good as the cops claim you are."

"The little girl is the daughter of one of our guys," Sam said nervously. "She was never in any real danger, Sandy. But we needed you to believe that she was."

"You frightened a little child for no reason?" Sandy cried out angrily. "What would make you do something so horrible, Sam? What kind of a monster—"

"For a large chunk of money," Kemp said. "That's why the cops did it. For enough money to buy a lot of equipment this department badly needs."

Sandy looked at Sam. He stared down at the floor. She could sense his shame. At the same time, she got a vivid picture in her mind of new computers and up-to-date lab equipment.

"Don't blame Sam," Kemp went on. "He just followed orders. If you want to blame someone, blame MiraMed and my employer—Jonathan Wolfe."

"I think it was a pretty low trick," Sandy said to Kemp. "Like bribery." She turned back to Sam. "Isn't that kind of thing against the law? Shouldn't you be arresting this man?"

Sam looked so miserable that Sandy almost felt sorry for him. She sighed. "Okay, I won't say any more."

She stared at Kemp. "Well, now that you've had your demonstration, I hope you're happy," she snapped. "And if that's all, I think—"

"Sandy, wait!" Sam cried. "There *has* been a crime. And we really do need your help!"

Chapter 5

Kemp insisted that they go out for something to eat. "You must be starved," he said to Sandy.

She was, although she hated to admit it. Finally, she agreed to have dinner with Kemp—as long as Sam came along, too. "You said that there was a crime involved," she told Sam. "I want to hear about it from a cop."

Sandy was not happy when Kemp picked a very expensive restaurant. She didn't want to feel she owed him for anything. But she knew she couldn't afford to eat here. "Can't we just grab a burger?" she asked. "I have a lot of homework waiting for me."

"Mr. Wolfe is meeting us here," Kemp explained. "He wants to talk to you in person about this case."

Sandy swallowed back resentment. These two strangers—Kemp and Wolfe—had been so sure of her, they'd made dinner reservations in advance!

As she followed Kemp across the restaurant, Sandy felt out of place. She could feel people staring as she walked by. No one else was wearing jeans and a cotton shirt, but Kemp didn't seem to notice. Or if he did, he didn't care.

The host showed them to an elegant private dining room. A large round table there was set with a heavy linen tablecloth and shining silverware. Just overhead hung a crystal chandelier. At one end of the room was a roaring fire in a huge stone fireplace.

A tall man dressed in jeans, a western shirt, and cowboy boots stood in front of the crackling fire. So who was this? The only thing missing from the picture, Sandy decided, was a ten-gallon hat. When Kemp introduced the cowboy as Jonathan Wolfe, Sandy's jaw dropped.

Wolfe turned all his attention on Sandy. It was almost as if Sam and Eric Kemp didn't exist. Sandy was a little amused by it. She sensed that Wolfe wanted to make a good impression on her, but she couldn't figure out why.

All during dinner, Sandy studied the mysterious Jonathan Wolfe. The cowboy-businessman was long and lanky, and he talked with a Texas accent. He didn't look like the kind of person who ran a huge company. Sandy had heard of MiraMed, but she wasn't sure what the company produced.

Wolfe insisted that they enjoy this dinner before talking business. Over dessert, he said to her, "Ms. Norris—"

"Please call me Sandy," she said with a smile. In spite of herself she found that she liked the boyish businessman as much as she disliked Eric Kemp. "Will you tell me now about the crime that has been committed?"

Wolfe smiled. "It's a theft, Sandy. The theft of a priceless formula that could save millions of lives."

Between them, Jonathan Wolfe and Sam Kennedy told Sandy the story. MiraMed produced medical products, including state-of-the-art drugs. Wolfe said that he and his partner, Greg Dixon, had founded MiraMed.

"Greg and I met in college," Wolfe drawled. "He was a science major, and I was studying business. It was the perfect combination."

After graduating, the two bright young men had pooled their talents and resources to start the company. Wolfe's father had helped them raise the money they needed.

"Greg never seemed to be interested in the money part of things," Wolfe said, pushing his chair back from the table. "As the company grew, we had to hire other scientists. Greg seemed perfectly happy to let someone else take care of hiring and firing. All he cared about was what he could see under a microscope."

"But all that changed a couple of months back," Sam cut in. "It seems that one of the other scientists came up with a cure for a disease called Ryse Virus."

"Ryse Virus strikes young children— mostly kids living in poverty," Wolfe explained. "Until recently, there was no cure. If a child became ill with the virus, well . . ." He shook his head sadly.

"But you say that your company had found a cure," Sandy said.

Wolfe smiled and nodded. "This new drug means that children will no longer have to die from this horrible disease. We were just getting ready to start production for public use. And then— *disaster!*"

Chapter 6

"The formula was stolen," Kemp said, "by Greg Dixon."

Sandy frowned. "How do you know Dixon stole it? And why would he?"

Wolfe chuckled and shook his head. "Sandy, it's easy to see that you know very little about the *business* end of medicine. There's a whole lot of money involved in keeping folks healthy."

"This is what happened, Sandy. Dixon and the formula disappeared at the same time," Sam explained. "Mr. Wolfe hired private detectives who tracked Dixon to another country—one not so friendly to us. We're pretty sure that Dixon is hiding out there."

"Why didn't you go to the police in the first place?" Sandy asked. "Or you could have called the FBI, or—"

Wolfe looked uncomfortable. "To be honest, we wanted to keep this thing quiet. We were afraid if we went to the cops or the feds, the whole world would find out."

"Huh? I don't understand. What does Dixon want to *do* with the formula?" Sandy asked. "I would have thought he'd be happy to save—"

"Obviously he plans to sell the formula," Kemp cut in, "to the highest bidder. He'll make a fortune."

Sandy looked from one man to another. "So you're saying that another company will buy the formula from Dixon. . . . " she said slowly.

Wolfe nodded. "Count on it. Unless we can get it back somehow."

Sandy gazed at Wolfe thoughtfully. "Is this where I come in?"

Wolfe leaned forward and stared intently into her eyes. "Sandy, I can't *tell* you how much we need your help. We want you to use your psychic abilities to track down the formula. It's the only way we can stop this horrible disease from killing anymore babies."

He reached out and took her hand. At that moment, Sandy felt a rush of confused feelings. For an instant, she "saw"—in her head—a strange vision. It was a clear, lifelike image of a young man with a tangle of long dark hair. He wore thick glasses and a shirt striped with wild colors.

But then Wolfe pulled his hand back and the image disappeared. "Will you help us?" Wolfe asked earnestly.

Sandy was silent for a moment. She wasn't sure how she felt about Wolfe. But she knew that Sam Kennedy was an honest and dependable cop. If Sam wanted her help, she'd gladly give it.

"I have a few questions," Sandy said to Wolfe. "Why didn't you just contact me to begin with? Why go to all the trouble of having the cops set up a fake missing child case? Why have Kemp spy on me? Why bribe the cops?"

"Whoa, girl!" Wolfe laughed, pushing his chair back. "First of all, we are *not* bribing the cops. The word you want is *reward*. And I promise you, Sandy—no matter what you decide to do—MiraMed will make that donation."

Sandy smiled. "Okay, fair enough. But tell me why—"

Wolfe interrupted her question. "As for the rest of it, we had to be absolutely certain that you could be trusted."

Sandy's eyebrows shot up. It had never occurred to her that anyone might question her integrity! But then she thought about all the phony psychics around. Wolfe was just being smart to check her out.

Wolfe frowned. "There's one thing, though. If you come to work for me, you will never be able to talk about what you did," he said. "Do you understand?"

"I don't usually talk about the cases I

work on," Sandy said coldly. Wolfe's statement had annoyed her. What did he think she was going to do—solve the case and go on a talk show? "Let's get this straight," Sandy said. "I'm not coming to work *for* you, Mr. Wolfe. If I agree to help you, I'll do this one job and that's it. And I won't accept any pay for my work."

Sam chuckled. "That's what I told them, kid. But I don't think these business-types believed me."

"Think about it, Sandy!" Wolfe exclaimed. "Don't you realize I could help you pay off all your college loans?"

Sandy smiled. "That's a happy thought. But I do my work for other reasons. Let this be my way of helping to get rid of Ryse Virus."

Wolfe nodded, but Sandy could tell that he didn't like it. She wondered if he thought he could control her through money. She sensed that Wolfe was that kind of person. Underneath his boyish grin and drawl, Jonathan Wolfe was a very tough guy who knew how to use money like a weapon.

"All right," Sandy said at last. "I'll help you get the formula."

Sandy and Jonathan Wolfe agreed on a time to meet the next day. Then Kemp drove Sam and Sandy back to the police station. As Kemp drove away, Sandy turned to Sam. "I don't know why those guys are making such a big deal about secrecy," she said. "It's not like I'm going to break into Fort Knox or something."

Sam took both of her hands in his. "Now you listen to me, kid," he said seriously. "There's a good reason why you need to keep quiet about your work. There's a *fortune* at stake here! Believe me, Dixon will do anything to keep the formula. Do you understand?"

Sandy gazed silently into the old cop's eyes. "Are you warning me that I could be in danger?"

Sam nodded. "That is *exactly* what I'm doing!"

Chapter 7

The next day, Sam picked up Sandy after her last class. He drove her to Jonathan Wolfe's home, a huge mansion overlooking the city. Sandy had insisted that Sam be with her, even though Wolfe didn't seem to like the arrangement. But Sandy had no intention of being left alone for a second with Eric Kemp.

From the moment Sam's clunky old car turned in through the tall iron gates, Sandy felt uncomfortable. Something was not right—and she could *feel* it. But she couldn't pinpoint exactly what was bothering her.

Kemp met them at the front door and led them to a handsomely decorated office. Jonathan Wolfe was leaning against a huge desk. Wolfe greeted them warmly, but he seemed anxious to get right to work.

Sam took a seat in a corner of the room. Wolfe led Sandy to a small table and a comfortable chair.

"You'll have to tell me what you need," Wolfe said. "Lights on or off? Drapes open or closed?"

Sandy smiled. "The room is fine," she said. "But I have to know what to look for. I need you to show me a sample of the formula. And I'll need some blank paper and a pencil—in case I find the formula. Remember that this is all a *mental* process—I can't just pick up the papers and walk away."

Wolfe chuckled.

"Another thing," Sandy added. "I need something that belonged to Greg Dixon. It has to be something he touched or wore. That will help me to focus on him, on where he is."

Wolfe handed her a stack of papers. "These are some of Greg's notes about the formula. This is what you'll be looking for. Papers like these."

Sandy studied the pages for a minute. The notes appeared to be math formulas of some kind. They made no sense to her, but at least she had an idea of what she was after.

Wolfe handed her a pad of paper and a pencil. Then he gave her a faded bandana. "Greg wears his hair long," Wolfe said with a chuckle. "He used this bandana to tie his hair back off his face. He called it his good-luck bandana."

The moment that Sandy took the bandana, she had the same vision she'd had the day before—a young man with long hair, glasses, and a striped shirt. Sandy tried to stay with the vision as long as possible, but it disappeared.

She drew a deep breath. Time to concentrate. She closed her eyes and leaned back in the chair. "A beach," she murmured. "Warm sand, palm trees. Ocean waves breaking on the sand."

Sandy could sense Wolfe's excitement, but only faintly. In her mind, she was already "leaving" his office.

A moment later Sandy "stood" on the beautiful beach. In a way, it was like a dream. The colors were much brighter and clearer than in real life. She wanted to stand there for a while, just to take in the beauty of the place. But again, an uncomfortable feeling of something being *wrong* invaded her sense of peace.

Some 50 yards or so from the water stood a weatherbeaten little wooden house. A beach towel and several pieces of wet clothing were draped over a clothesline next to the house. Sandy saw the striped shirt waving in the breeze.

She moved toward the front steps. As if walking on air, Sandy glided to the front door. She saw that it was wide open. Inside she could see a few pieces of scarred old furniture. Sandy glided into the room.

On the far side of the room, Sandy

saw a young man lying on his side on a cot. He seemed to be asleep. She glided closer to the cot and leaned over him. It was Greg Dixon, all right—but Sandy's sense of something being wrong now grew even stronger.

She looked around the room. It was a mess. Obviously, Dixon wasn't much of a housekeeper. All over the floor, dirty clothes were mixed up with books, old newspapers, and dishes.

Where would Dixon have hidden the formula? Sandy glided from this room to the next. It turned out to be a grubby little kitchen. It, too, was a mess. The counters were dirty, and the drawers and cupboards had been left hanging open. She carefully searched the room, but found nothing.

Beyond the kitchen was the tiny bathroom. It looked even worse than the kitchen. Apparently, Greg had been doing some work on the plumbing. There was a bucket under the sink and a few tools lying around on the floor.

Sandy was about to turn away when suddenly she had a funny feeling about the sink. Now she took a closer look. Sure enough, something was hidden in the pipe. Sandy "looked" into the depths of the plumbing. Then she saw it. A piece of paper protected by plastic had been stuffed into the elbow pipe under the sink.

Sandy "read" the paper. Half the page was covered with numbers, letters, and strange-looking symbols. This surely couldn't be the whole formula!

"Wait," Sandy thought. "The messy house—" She glided back into the living room, gazing at the books on the floor. She forced herself to "see" into one of the books. Just as she had suspected, a tiny roll of paper was tucked into the spine. Sandy strained to "read" it. It was more of the formula!

In her excitement, Sandy's breathing quickened. Greg had separated the pages of the formula and hidden each one in a different place! But why leave the house in such a mess, unless—

Sandy glided back to the cot. Greg groaned and turned onto his back.

Sandy gasped when she looked at him. One side of his face was bruised black and blue! Sandy's heart sank. Somehow she knew for certain that Greg Dixon had *not* been hurt accidentally. He'd been badly beaten!

Chapter 8

Sandy felt her mind rushing back into her physical body. She opened her eyes, blinking at the light in the room. Sam was kneeling next to her chair. He looked worried. "Are you okay, kid?"

Sandy took a deep breath and nodded. Aside from feeling wrung out, she was fine. Then she noticed Jonathan Wolfe. He was gazing at the pad of paper she had been holding. Now Sandy saw that the pages were covered with scribbled marks. She must have written down the formula as she "read" it off the pages hidden in Dixon's cabin!

Kemp stood next to Wolfe, looking over his shoulder at the formula. Then, all of a sudden, Kemp looked directly at Sandy. His smile made Sandy shudder.

He looked exactly like a hungry shark!

"Can we go now?" she whispered to Sam. "I—I need to get out of here."

"Sure thing," Sam said. He helped her to her feet. Wolfe barely looked up from the formula as Kemp showed them to the door.

"I want you to know that the donation to the police department has already been made," Kemp told Sam. "I'm sure your people will be very happy with the new equipment."

"Thanks," Sam muttered. After the front door closed behind them, Sam wriggled uncomfortably. "Tell me something, Sandy. Why do I feel like I just waded through an open sewer?"

"Ugh," Sandy agreed with a shaky laugh. "I feel the same way. I don't know what it is about Kemp—but he almost makes me physically ill. There's something *evil* about that man."

"Well, it's over with," Sam said as they climbed into his car. "And for all I care, Dixon can rot in his new home. Or, to be more accurate—freeze!" Sam chuckled. "With winter coming on, he's going to be one cold, sorry character."

Sandy glanced at Sam with a puzzled frown. "*Freeze?* Not likely. He's hiding out in a tropical climate. What do you mean, Sam?" she asked.

"I told you before," Sam said. "Dixon escaped from the United States and flew to a country in Europe that—"

"No!" Sandy objected. "All you said was that it was a country that wasn't friendly with us."

"That's right," Sam said.

"You didn't say it was in Europe."

"Eastern Europe, to be exact," Sam said. "One of those Balkan countries—"

"No!" Sandy cried out. "Oh, Sam, no! If that's true, then—"

Sam pulled the car to the side of the road and stopped at the curb. "What's wrong with you, kid?"

"Sam, I think we've made a terrible

mistake," Sandy said. She was shaking all over. She couldn't rid herself of the memory of Greg Dixon, lying bruised and beaten on the shabby little cot.

Sam gazed at her in confusion. "Maybe you better tell me what's going on here," he growled.

At Sandy's insistence, they drove to a coffee shop. They chose a table on the far side of the patio. A waitress served them glasses of cold lemonade.

Sandy told Sam what she had seen from the very beginning. She could tell he was shocked by her story.

"Wolfe told us he'd hired private detectives to hunt Dixon down," Sam said. "He mentioned they'd tracked Dixon to Eastern Europe. There was no way we could touch Dixon there."

"Wolfe knew that," Sandy said bitterly. "He also knew you'd have to involve a psychic if you couldn't get to Dixon any other way."

"We had no reason not to believe

Jonathan Wolfe," Sam said bitterly.

"Plus the promise of a huge donation didn't hurt," Sandy said. When she saw the embarrassment and pain in Sam's eyes, she covered his hand with hers. "Sam, you did what you thought was right for the department. You couldn't have known what Wolfe was up to."

Sam groaned. "I don't know how he found out about your work, kid, but he knew all about it."

Sandy sighed. "He probably used his private detectives to talk to the families I've helped. Guys like Wolfe can buy anything they want, Sam—including information."

"But why would he lie about it?" Sam said in an annoyed voice. "I just don't get it."

Sandy looked into the depths of her glass. "Dixon is closer to the United States than Wolfe said. He's in a warm, tropical place, on a beach, close to—"

"Mexico?" Sam suggested.

Sandy thought about it. "You could be right," she said. "If so, Dixon is just a few hours from here. And Sam—he's been hurt. Someone beat him up."

Sam shook his head. "What? That means someone else must be after the formula!"

Suddenly, Sandy drew her breath in sharply. "No one else," she burst out. "I think I know what happened."

"Go on," Sam said.

"I think Wolfe's detectives found out where Dixon was hiding," Sandy said. "Kemp must have gone to Mexico to get the formula. But Greg had hidden each page in a different place. Kemp couldn't find all the pages. That's why he beat up Dixon. He tried to make him tell where the rest of the formula was. But Dixon refused, so Kemp left him there."

"Then they pulled *you* in to find the formula," Sam said. He clenched his fist and slammed it into the palm of his other hand. He was furious. "If I could just get my hands on that Kemp—"

"Please, no more violence," Sandy said. "Why can't you just arrest Kemp and Wolfe? They're *criminals*."

Sam shook his head. "I'm afraid not, Sandy. They haven't broken a single law—at least, not in this country."

Sandy put her head in her hands. "I can't believe that they used me to—" Then she gasped, her eyes widening.

"Sam, what if *everything* they told us was a lie? What if Dixon was the person who created the formula? What if I stole it from its rightful owner?"

Chapter 9

Sam and Sandy were lost in their own thoughts as they drove away from the coffee shop. Sam didn't say a word until he dropped Sandy off in front of her apartment building. "Don't give up, kid," he said. "Trust me. We'll find a way to make those two pay."

"How?" Sandy said. "They've got all that money and power to back them up, Sam! What do *we* have?"

Sam just shook his head and drove away. But the question continued to haunt Sandy. She felt helpless. How much could a young college student and an old detective do on their own?

Sandy didn't sleep well that night. She dreamed about Greg Dixon. In her dream, he was surrounded by children suffering from Ryse Virus. They pulled at his arms and tugged at his clothes, wailing at him for help. When Greg pointed at *her*, Sandy woke up in tears. She could hear herself crying out, "I'm sorry! I'm sorry!"

After her shower, Sandy took her breakfast into the living room. She turned on the TV. Maybe the noise and the pictures would block out the terrible sounds and sights of the dying children. She was just spooning sugar on a big bowl of cornflakes when a news item caught her attention.

MiraMed had announced that it had found a cure for the dreaded Ryse Virus. As soon as the FDA approved the drug, the announcer said, it would go on the market. The new drug, however, was going to be expensive.

As Sandy listened in horror, she saw a film clip of Jonathan Wolfe being interviewed. "What about the children in third-world countries?" he was asked.

"We're all concerned, of course. It's a real shame that the development cost of this drug was so high," Wolfe drawled. "We'll do our best to keep the cost down—but we have expenses, too."

"Will you be willing to share this discovery with other drug companies?" the commentator asked.

Wolfe smiled, but there was no warmth in his face. "Well, unfortunately, that would cheat our stockholders. Our first duty is to them," he said. "After all, we have to make some small profit."

Without thinking, Sandy jumped to her feet. Bowl, cornflakes, sugar, and milk went flying out in all directions. "You *liar!*" she roared.

Then she realized that yelling at the television set wouldn't accomplish anything. "We need to talk to Greg Dixon," she thought to herself. "I have to find out what *really* happened. Then maybe I can figure out a way to undo the damage. This is all my fault, and—"

Sandy gasped. All of a sudden she knew *exactly* what a young college student and an old detective could do!

She cleaned up the remains of her breakfast. Then she sat down and closed her eyes, forcing herself to focus on an image of Greg Dixon.

Sandy went deeper and deeper into a trance state. Once again she was on that sunny beach. This time she took a few minutes to get a good look around. There were fishing nets spread out to dry on a pile of rocks. In the distance she could see small boats rising and falling in the waves. A fishing village?

Sandy glided into the cabin. It was no longer a mess. All the clothes, books, and newspapers had been picked up and put away. The cot was neatly made—but Greg Dixon was nowhere in sight.

Then Sandy saw a newspaper lying on the wooden table. A photo of Jonathan Wolfe dominated the front page. But the caption was written in another language. Sandy studied the scene carefully. She forced herself to look closely so she would remember the name of the newspaper.

She was about to leave the cabin when a shadow fell across the floor. Greg Dixon! Sandy was so startled to see him that she snapped out of her trance. She came awake abruptly. For a moment she just sat in the kitchen chair, shaking from head to toe. Then she made herself remember where she had been.

The newspaper had been written in Spanish, but Sandy had no idea where the fishing village was. It could have been in Mexico or Central America or even somewhere in South America. "Or maybe the shores of sunny Spain," she thought, "or Puerto Rico or—"

She sighed and reached for the phone. A call to the library gave her the information she needed. The newspaper she named was published in a small coastal town in northern Mexico.

Sandy phoned Sam to tell him what she'd learned. "We've got to get to Greg Dixon," she said. "I'm glad he's all right. But I have a funny feeling he may try to get that formula away from Wolfe."

"You know what will happen if Kemp decides that Dixon is a threat. Next time, Kemp won't stop at just a beating," Sam growled. "You know I'm right, Sandy. He'll do whatever it takes to get Dixon out of the picture."

Sandy felt a cold chill. "You mean he'd *kill* Greg Dixon?" she whispered.

"You got it, kid," Sam said. "Look, I know where that village is. We can drive there in a few hours. I hate to ask you to miss any of your classes, but—"

"No problem. Pick me up in half an hour," Sandy said.

"Here's another thought," Sam said. "Dixon may *not* plan to go after Wolfe and Kemp. He may have already figured out that they have no use for him now. If he's smart, he's already on the run.

So don't forget to pack your handy-dandy psychic locator."

Sandy chuckled. "Consider it done."

"Another thing," Sam said, all humor now gone from his voice. "The same threat applies to you and me, Sandy. Let's face it—Wolfe and Kemp don't need *us*, either. In fact, it may be to their advantage to get rid of us for good. So you'd better watch your back!"

Sandy had a sudden flash of memory. She saw a bucket of ice cubes dumped down her back. But what was *that* image all about? Was it a psychic warning of some kind?

Chapter 10

It was late afternoon by the time Sam and Sandy reached the little Mexican fishing village. It took them a while to find someone who knew where Greg's cabin was. By the time they arrived, the sun was hanging low on the horizon.

As Sam parked on the road above the beach, Sandy gazed at the view. Any other time she would have wanted to stay right here. She always loved to watch the sun go down on the ocean. It was beautiful—as if a great artist had taken the colors of the sunset and poured them across the dark blue waves.

"Come on," Sam growled. "Let's not waste time."

Sandy felt very strange, knocking on Dixon's front door. Twice before she had visited—yet she had never actually set foot in the place! "Greg Dixon will never forgive me for what I did," she thought sadly, "and I don't blame him."

Suddenly the door opened wide. She found herself standing face-to-face with her so-called victim. "Yes?" Greg said.

Sandy could only stutter, so Sam broke in. He explained who they were and why they had come.

Partway through the explanation, Greg stood aside and let them in. He took the wobbly chair and Sam sat on the cot. Sandy didn't want to sit. Instead, she looked out the window. She watched the sunset, feeling worse and worse as Sam told their story.

"You're saying that *you* stole the formula from me?" Greg exclaimed. "But *how?*" Sandy turned. He was staring at her as if he thought she was a freak. She sighed. She'd seen that look on the faces of other people.

"I don't suppose you know what

'remote viewing' is?" she asked. Greg shrugged. "I've heard of it, but I never believed in it," he said. "Are you telling me you're a psychic?"

"I'm afraid so," she said. "And I can tell you all the places where you hid the formula." When she saw Greg Dixon wince, she knew exactly what he was thinking. "You were clever to hide each page in a different place. Tell me, was it Kemp who beat you up?"

Greg touched the bruises on his face and nodded. "Yeah, it was Kemp, all right. He specializes in that kind of thing. The truth is that *I* invented the formula to begin with. I was so excited the day I knew for sure that the formula worked. I had visions of curing all the children who were dying of Ryse Virus. The vaccine would be a gift to the world from MiraMed!"

Sam snorted. "But Wolfe had other ideas?" he asked.

Greg nodded. "Money, money, and

more money. And it's not as if he *needs* it! He's so rich now he'll never be able to spend it all."

"So you fled to Mexico," Sandy said.

"I used to come down here on school vacations," Greg said. "This little town is a great place to fish, to swim, to take walks on the beach." He smiled. "When we were in college, Jonathan came down here with me a few times. In fact, it was here that we got the idea of going into business together. That's how MiraMed got started."

By now, the last rays of daylight had disappeared. Greg got up to switch on a lamp, but Sam stopped him. "Light would make us easy targets," Sam growled. "We need to get out of here right away. Let's go some place where Wolfe and Kemp can't find us."

They piled into Sam's car and traveled about 10 miles down the road. Then Greg suddenly remembered that the formula was still in the cottage. "I can't believe I forgot it," he said. "That's my work! Even though Kemp and Wolfe have a copy of it, I still have the original. We have to go back and get it."

Sam sighed heavily. "Okay, okay! But when we get back to the cabin, we get in and out as quickly as possible."

They had just turned onto the road that led down to the beach when Sam slammed on the brakes. He pointed through the windshield at a bright glow in the sky. At first Sandy didn't know what she was looking at. But then the unmistakable odor of smoke reached her nostrils. *"Fire!"* she gasped.

"The formula!" Greg howled.

Sam turned the steering wheel as fast as he could, hit the gas, and sped away.

"No, Sam! You have to go back," Greg cried out. "I might be able to—"

"You still don't get it, do you?" Sam growled. "You *can't* go back! Not unless you want to die."

Chapter 11

Sam drove straight to the border. All along the way, Sandy noticed that he kept glancing into the rearview mirror. Finally, when he was sure they weren't being followed, he began to relax.

"We aren't staying in Mexico," he told Sandy and Greg. "Whoever set the cabin on fire may have thought Greg was still in there. I don't want anyone to know where he is right now."

"So where *do* we go?" Greg asked. "And what do we have to do to get Wolfe and Kemp behind bars?"

"We don't," Sam said. "Look, Greg, you and Wolfe were both employees of MiraMed. When you stole that formula from the company, you broke the law!"

"Me? Broke the law?"

"That's right," Sam said. "And if Wolfe finds out you're back in the United States, he might press charges."

"But Kemp tried to kill me!" Greg exclaimed. "And the fire—"

"There's not a shred of proof that Wolfe's men set the fire," Sam said. "And as for that beating, it's only your word against his. Besides, it didn't happen in the United States."

Greg slumped back against the seat. He looked defeated.

"Wolfe's going to make a lot of money. And sick kids who are too poor to pay for the drug will go on dying," Greg said sadly. "That's why I took the formula. After all, *I'm* the one who discovered the cure!"

"But it belongs to MiraMed," Sam said patiently. "You know, Greg, you should have paid closer attention to the business side of your company."

"So what are you saying? Have I lost everything?" Greg groaned.

"Maybe not," Sam said with a chuckle. "I've got an idea that might solve several of our problems."

When he outlined his plan, Sandy and Greg were eager to get started. Then Sam told Sandy what part she would play. "Sam, you *know* how much I hate publicity!" she objected. "I can't believe you want me to do this."

"Listen, kid, I wish there was another way," Sam growled. "But there isn't."

"Come on, Sandy—please say you'll do it," Greg begged. "Think of the kids who will benefit."

Sandy sighed. "All right," she finally agreed. "But you guys had better be with me the whole time."

They arrived back in the city just a few hours before dawn. Sam turned onto Sandy's street and started to slow down in front of her apartment building. But at the last minute, he suddenly sped up and drove on by.

"You've got company," Sam said in

his gravelly voice. "There's somebody in a dark car parked right in front of the building."

"So what?" Sandy said. "You don't know—"

"It has a MiraMed logo on the door."

"One of the company cars," Greg said. "But why—"

"I don't know," Sam snapped. "The point is, this is a strange time of day to go visiting, wouldn't you say?"

"What do you think they want?" Sandy asked in a trembling voice.

"Again, I don't know." Sam checked the rearview mirror several times as he whipped up and down streets. "But I have a pretty good idea. Wolfe and Kemp probably don't want any loose ends—if you know what I mean."

"Oh, no! Do you suppose there's a welcoming committee at my place, too?" Greg said.

"It won't take long to find out," Sam said. "What's your address, Greg?"

They drove to Greg's house on the west side of the city. Sandy was surprised to discover that Greg lived in a modest neighborhood of small frame houses. Then she realized why. Greg Dixon hadn't let the success of the business destroy his values.

Sam parked up the street. "Wait here," he told Greg and Sandy. "I want to check the place out. We wouldn't want to be surprised by a welcoming committee." He climbed out of the car, disappearing into the shadows.

He was back in less than five minutes. "We've got to get out of here," he said. "Eric Kemp himself is waiting for you, Greg. Given what we know about Kemp, I wouldn't say he dropped by for tea and crumpets."

Sandy stifled nervous laughter as Sam started the car. "Then where *do* we go?"

"Yeah," Greg said. "I don't suppose there's any use in checking out your house, Sam. They'll be watching that, too. And no offense—but I don't want to spend the rest of my life in your car!"

Sam grinned. "What would be the safest place in the city?"

"Maybe the police department?" Sandy asked.

Sam laughed. "Actually, I think we can use the precinct safe house." To Greg, he added, "That's where cops hold witnesses to keep them secure until they can testify. We've got a safe house near here. Nothing fancy, but I doubt that Kemp and his men know about it."

After they settled down in the safe house, Sam called the precinct and talked to his captain.

When he hung up, Sandy said, "Help me out, Sam. There's one thing I don't understand. If Wolfe has the formula, why is he still after us?"

"It's Greg they want," Sam said, "not you or me. But if my plan works, we'll *all* be off the hook!"

Chapter 12

Three days later, a dozen reporters were invited to a press conference at police headquarters. The police chief wanted to thank Jonathan Wolfe for his generous donation. Sandy hadn't been sure that Wolfe would come to the conference. But the glory-hungry businessman couldn't resist the photo opportunity.

The conference was held in a large meeting room with a small stage. Sam, Sandy, and Greg were waiting offstage in a side room, where Wolfe and Kemp wouldn't see them.

After welcoming Jonathan Wolfe to the microphone, the captain told the reporters what Wolfe's donation meant. "We're buying new lab equipment," he said with a big grin, "and several more computers. Mr. Wolfe's generosity has made our work a whole lot easier."

Wolfe looked pleased. He made a short speech about how important it was to help the police with their work.

Then the captain said, "And now I'd like to bring out someone else who has made a very important donation to the department."

When Sandy stepped onstage, Wolfe looked surprised to see her. But he forced a smile as she approached.

The captain explained to the audience that Sandy helped find people who were lost or missing. "She's donated her time over the years," the captain said. "To be honest, though, I still have a hard time with this psychic stuff." Everyone laughed. "But the fact is that Sandy has found missing people we'd given up on. She's saved many lives." There was more applause.

Sandy's heart was pounding. This

was her cue. Determined to stay calm, she stepped up to the microphone. She hoped that nerves wouldn't make her voice sound shaky. What she had to say was too important.

She looked directly at Jonathan Wolfe. "Saving the lives of children makes it all worthwhile," she said. "I'm sure Mr. Wolfe agrees with me on that!"

Wolfe nodded. "Absolutely!" he said with a wide smile.

"You have another announcement to make, don't you, Mr. Wolfe?" Sandy went on. The smile faded from Wolfe's eyes. "Now that you have the formula to cure Ryse Virus, I want to thank you in advance for dropping the price for children who can't afford it."

Wolfe's smile was shaky, threatening to vanish altogether.

"Your partner, Greg Dixon, has already leaked the news," Sandy said.

Wolfe froze.

"Well, I, uh—" He stumbled.

Sandy forced a big smile.

Then Greg stepped out on the stage. When Wolfe saw his partner, his face turned gray. Greg stepped up to the microphone, and Sandy made sure she was standing between the two men. It didn't take psychic powers to feel the waves of tension between them.

"When Jonathan and I first started MiraMed," Greg told the members of the press, "we had a wonderful vision. We wanted to use our skills to make the world a better place. Over the years, thanks to Jonathan, the company has been very successful. All of us at MiraMed have gotten rich. Keeping the price low for our Ryse Virus drug is our way of sharing our good fortune with our community. Isn't it, Jon?"

Wolfe's smile was strained. He didn't seem able to trust himself to speak.

"As of today, I'm leaving MiraMed to work on my own research projects," Greg said. "But I'm proud and happy that Jonathan will be staying true to the vision we first had."

"And I'll *see* to it that he does," Sandy said with a big grin. "With my gift, I can see more than meets the eye!"

The reporters laughed at her silliness, but she could tell that Jonathan had gotten the message. He might not be happy about it, but he would have to leave Greg alone. Best of all, he would make the drug affordable. He *had* to! He'd never know when Sandy was using her second sight to watch him.

Greg turned and walked offstage. Sandy knew that Sam was hustling him out of the building. Greg had already arranged to work for another drug company in a distant city.

As the press conference ended, the reporters surrounded Wolfe, peppering him with questions. When Sandy slipped offstage, Sam was waiting for her in the wings. "You did great, kid," he said with a chuckle. "You better believe Wolfe's going to have to toe the line now."

"Do you think he'll try to come after me?" Sandy asked. "You know—try to get even with me for what I just did?"

Sam shook his head. "Not a chance. You're way too visible now. That was the whole point of this press conference. You may have the press hounding you— but you're safe, kid. Believe me!"

Sandy breathed a sigh of relief. "That's good, Sam, because I am *not* ready to give harp lessons to the angels."

COMPREHENSION QUESTIONS

RECALL

1. What was Sandy Norris's "special gift"?

2. Why did the police deceive Sandy about looking for a lost child?

3. Why was it so hard to find the entire formula for the new drug?

4. As Sandy went into a trance, what object belonging to Greg Dixon did she hold in her hand?

IDENTIFYING CHARACTERS

1. Who had a vision of curing all the children infected by Ryse Virus?

2. Who told the reporters that he couldn't forget his responsibility to his stockholders?

3. Who was impressed by Sandy's refusal to take money for finding missing people?